CLASSIC FAIRY TALES

READER'S DIGEST YOUNG FAMILIES, INC.

Cover and title page illustrated by Kathy Mitchell

This edition is published by Reader's Digest Young Families, Inc.

Pleasantville, NY 10570

www.readersdigest.com

Reader's Digest Young Families is a trademark of The Reader's Digest Association, Inc.

Louis Weber, C.E.O.

Publications International, Ltd.

7373 North Cicero Avenue

Lincolnwood, Illinois 60712

www.pubint.com

Manufactured in China.

8 7 6 5 4 3 2 1

ISBN: 0-7853-4742-9

CONTENTS

The Wild Swans

Adapted by Brian Conway
Illustrated by Kathy Mitchell

Once there was a king who had happiness and great fortune. Of all his treasures, he was proudest of his four children, the most perfect children in the land. His three fine, strong sons would do anything for their father, and the king's greatest joy, his daughter Elise, was clearly the dearest, sweetest, and most beautiful child in all the world.

Elise spent much of her time in her garden. Next to her brothers and her father, her lovely roses were Elise's greatest treasures. She would spend hour after hour caring for them.

Then one day the king hurried to find Elise. He was very worried. "I have terrible news," he told her. "You are in danger."

The king had many treasures, it is true, but for this he also had many wicked and powerful enemies. They were evil sorcerers and magicians who believed no one should have as much happiness as the king did.

"I fear for your safety," the king told his daughter. "You must go away from me now."

"But, Father," Elise sobbed, "I want to stay with you and my brothers."

The king sighed. "Your brothers have been taken away from us," he sadly told her. "I know not where. I cannot stand to lose you, too."

The king told the sweet princess to go with his trusted servants, who would take her to safety in their home in the forest. He said he might never see her again.

"When you're old enough," said the king, "find your brothers and come back to me."

He kissed her good-bye. Elise did as her father said. She lived hidden away in the servants' house for many years. She was treated well, but she was very unhappy. The sadness was unbearable as Elise longed to see her three beloved brothers again.

When Elise was old enough, she set off in search of her brothers. She had no idea where to look, but she knew in her heart they were still alive, and something inside told her they needed her help.

After several days of wandering and hoping for some sign, Elise met an old woman picking berries in the forest.

"I am looking for my three brothers," Elise told the woman. "They are fine, strong princes. Have you seen them?"

"I have seen nothing all day but three white swans with golden crowns on their heads," the old woman replied. "They were sunning themselves on the shore."

She directed Elise to the spot. There, Elise found three white feathers. She clutched them close to her and fell asleep while she waited for the swans to return.

Just before sunset, Elise woke up to see three majestic swans gliding down to the shore. They landed beside her, and, as the last ray of sunshine disappeared over the sea, the three swans changed magically into three princes. Elise was overjoyed to see her brothers again. It had been years since they laid eyes on each other. They held her close and told her what had happened to them.

On that day many years ago, an evil sorcerer had come to the castle. He found Elise's brothers in the stables. This sorcerer vowed to ruin the king's happiness, which he did the moment he turned the three princes into swans. They had lived apart from their father since then as swans during the day. At nightfall the soft rays of moonlight made them human again. The sorcerer had planned to cast a spell on Elise, too, but luckily she had escaped him.

"We have looked for you for several years," the eldest brother told Elise. "But you were very well hidden."

"We have flown to see our father," the second brother told Elise. "He is safe, but terribly unhappy. He now serves the sorcerer."

"He cannot help us," added the third brother. "But each day he makes a wish on a dried rosebud. He wishes we will find each other and make things right again."

Elise promised to help free her brothers from the sorcerer's wicked spell. Her brothers told her of an enchanted land far across the sea where they might find a way to break the spell.

"Take me with you," Elise urged them. "I know I can help you."

Her brothers prepared a net to carry their sister. The next morning the sun's rays turned them into swans again. They flew high above the sea, carrying Elise as she slept.

After two days' flight, they arrived at the kingdom across the sea. It was a beautiful kingdom of goodness and kindness. It was said that the Fairy Queen Morgana lived there. Surely she would know how to help them.

Elise's brothers found her a cave to rest in while they searched for Morgana from the skies. As Elise fell asleep there, she wished for a way to free her brothers from the spell. Even in her dreams, Elise prayed for help.

That night Queen Morgana came to Elise in a dream. Elise knew her! She was the woman who Elise had seen picking berries in the woods just a few days before.

"Only you can free your brothers," Morgana whispered to Elise. "But you must sacrifice greatly."

"I will," Elise promised. Then she listened carefully to the Fairy Queen's instructions. "Take the things you treasure most," Morgana said, "and craft three shirts, one for each brother. This task may take a very long time, but when you cover the swans with the shirts made from what you love, the spell will forever be broken."

"There is one more thing," Morgana added. "You may not speak until the shirts are made. If you do, your words will pierce your brothers' hearts like arrows."

With that, Morgana disappeared. Elise awoke with a start to find that the cave in which she slept was surrounded with hundreds of lovely rose-bushes, like the ones she'd had as a child.

She touched the roses. Yes, they were real. She was no longer dreaming. Elise set to work immediately, as Morgana had directed. Elise picked rose after rose and plucked petal after petal. She used the roses' prickly thorns as needles to string the petals together.

For twelve days, Elise worked without rest. The thought of saving her brothers gave her strength to continue.

On the thirteenth day Elise began sewing the third shirt when a woodcutter and his wife came upon Elise's rose garden.

"Here are the roses I told you about, my dear," the woodcutter called to his wife. "They sprung up over night."

Her eyes grew large. The woodcutter's wife loved roses, too. She leaned forward for a closer look, and saw Elise working there among the petals.

"What are you doing in the woods alone?" they asked, but Elise didn't dare speak, out of fear for her brothers' lives. "Poor child, come with us. We'll give you proper food and rest."

Elise struggled against the woodcutter. She was grateful, but she could not speak to tell them why she resisted. She thought only of her brothers.

Elise gathered up the shirts and as many roses as she could carry. Then she went sadly with the woodcutter and his wife. Elise feared she would never see her rose garden again.

Elise stayed with the couple for many days and did as the woodcutter and his wife asked. At night, though, she would stay awake to finish the last shirt. Before long, Elise ran out of rose petals. She needed at least one more blooming rosebush to finish the shirt.

The next day Elise found what she needed in the woodcutter's garden. There his wife kept her prized roses. Elise crept out of the house that night and plucked the petals from the roses, then began sewing. At sunrise, she had one cuff left to sew as the woodcutter's wife stormed into the garden.

"Ungrateful girl!" she shouted. "You've ruined my roses!"

Flying the skies in search of some sign of their sister, Elise's brothers heard the shouts of the woodcutter's wife.

They flew to the house and landed in the garden. They squawked at the woodcutter and his wife, who ran away in fear. Elise quickly spread the three shirts over the swans.

Before her eyes, the swans became men again.

Elise, anxious to speak now that the spell had been broken, explained everything to the woodcutter and his wife. "I'm sorry that I have been so difficult, when you have been so kind," said Elise. "My brothers and I thank you. We will repay you this moment."

Elise and her brothers brought all the rosebushes from the forest cave and planted them in the garden behind the woodcutter's house. Elise and her brothers sent for their father the very next day. A flock of ten wild swans delivered a message of joy. The king now had the strength and desire to escape the evil sorcerer. Soon the family was reunited. Elise and her brothers prepared a new castle for their father, who became the king of a new land.

Of course, Elise's brothers remembered to plant a rose garden on the castle grounds. It is said that this rose garden is where Elise weaves the most fragrant and lovely rosebushes by hand and sends a flock of wild swans to plant them in forests all over the world.

Thumbelina

Adapted by Megan Musgrave
Illustrated by Jane Maday

There was once a woman who lived in a tiny cottage which had the most beautiful garden in the world. She was very happy tending her garden, but over time she became sad. She had no children who could share her garden with her. She decided to visit the old witch in her village and ask for her help.

When the woman explained that she wanted a child, the old witch thought for a moment. Then she pulled a tiny bag out of a fold in her cloak. "Plant these wildflower seeds and tend them carefully every day. Soon you will have your wish," said the old witch.

The woman took the seeds home with her. The next day, she planted them in a sunny corner of her garden. She watered them and watched over them carefully. Days passed and the woman waited anxiously for her wish to come true.

Soon tiny green sprouts began to poke up out of the ground. Before long, the sprouts grew and blossomed into a beautiful patch of wildflowers.

In the center of the wildflower patch grew a single, beautiful tulip. Its deep pink petals were closed up tightly. The flower was so lovely that the woman could not resist bending down to smell it. As she knelt in front of the flower, its petals suddenly opened. The woman was amazed to find a tiny girl sitting inside the open tulip. She wore a tulip petal for a dress and had long, gleaming hair.

"You are the most beautiful child I have ever seen! And you are hardly even as big as my thumb. Would you like to stay with me in my garden?" asked the woman.

"Oh, yes!" replied the tiny girl.

"I will call you Thumbelina," said the woman. She made Thumbelina a tiny bed out of a shiny acorn shell. The tiny girl slept soundly, kept warm by her rose petal blanket.

Thumbelina and her mother lived very happily in the garden the whole summer long. Thumbelina loved to play in the little pond in the middle of the garden, so her mother made her a tiny boat out of a maple leaf. Thumbelina rowed around the pond, using two blades of grass as oars. Her mother sat by the side of the pond and read stories to her while she played. The two were so happy together.

Sometimes, Thumbelina sang as she rowed. She had a beautiful, silvery voice that her mother always loved to hear.

One day, a frog was hopping by the garden. He heard Thumbelina's beautiful voice and came near the pond. When he saw the tiny girl rowing her maple leaf boat he said, "I've never seen such a beautiful creature! I must take her away to my lily pad to be my wife."

The frog watched and waited until Thumbelina's mother went inside the cottage to get a cup of lemonade for Thumbelina. Then the frog jumped out from behind the reeds where he had been hiding and captured Thumbelina. He carried her away to the river where he lived and placed her on a lily pad. "Rest here while I go and make the plans for our wedding," said the frog. With that, he hopped away.

Thumbelina did not want to be the wife of a frog. She thought of her mother's beautiful garden. More than anything she wanted to be at home with her mother again. She became so sad that she began to cry. Her tiny tears fell into the river and made ripples in its glassy surface.

When the fish in the river saw Thumbelina crying, they decided to help her. They nibbled through the stem of her lily pad until it broke free and floated down the river, far away from the frog.

Thumbelina flowed gently on the river until finally the lily pad came to rest on a green, grassy bank of the river.

Thumbelina climbed up the bank and found herself on the edge of a grassy meadow. "This will be a fine place for me to live until I can find my way back to Mother again," she said.

She wove herself a tiny hammock out of grass blades and hung it up beneath a large daisy which sheltered her from the dew at night. During the day she wandered through the beautiful meadow nearby. If she was thirsty, she drank the dew off a blade of grass. If she was hungry, she had a bite of clover or some honeysuckle. She became friends with the butterflies and ladybugs and other creatures on the meadow, and at night she slept safely under her daisy roof.

One day, Thumbelina noticed that the days were getting chilly. The flowers of the meadow were fading, and the leaves were turning bright shades of orange, red, and yellow and dropping from the trees. Fall was coming. Soon so many leaves were falling that it was all Thumbelina could do to keep out from under them.

The nights were becoming colder, too. She made herself a blanket out of cotton from the meadow, but soon it was not enough to keep her warm at night. "How will I keep warm in the winter?" cried Thumbelina. She began to take long walks, looking for a place where she could be safe and warm for the winter. One day, she found a small burrow inside a tree. She poked her head inside to see if anyone lived there.

Inside the little burrow lived a friendly old field mouse. The burrow was snug and cozy, for the mouse had lined it with cotton and hay from the meadow nearby.

"Excuse me," said Thumbelina quietly. "May I come into your warm burrow for a moment?"

The old field mouse almost never had any visitors in autumn, and she was very happy to have one now.

"Come in, come in! You poor dear, you'll catch your death of cold. Come over by the fire and have a cup of tea."

Thumbelina and the field mouse were soon fast friends. The field mouse invited Thumbelina to stay with her for the winter. Together they gathered nuts, grains, and berries for the cold months ahead. Thumbelina sang songs and told her friend stories of her adventures, while the field mouse cooked their dinner or sewed by the fire.

One day it began to snow outside. Thumbelina had never seen snow before, so she opened the door of the burrow to peek outside. Some of the snowflakes were almost as big as she was! She loved to watch them dance in the air and come to rest gently on the ground. But as she watched the snow fall she saw something strange. Lying near the field mouse's front door was a young sparrow with a broken wing. He was shivering as the snow began to cover him.

Thumbelina called to the field mouse. Together they helped the sparrow into the burrow. After they fed him some soup, he was able to speak.

"I injured myself as my friends and I were flying south for the winter," chirped the sparrow. "I would have frozen to death if you hadn't found me. Thank you so very much."

Thumbelina, the sparrow, and the field mouse passed a wonderful winter together in the burrow. Thumbelina helped mend the sparrow's wing so that he would be able to fly again when spring came. She told stories about her mother and the wonderful garden where she was born.

One day, Thumbelina poked her head outside the burrow again. The snow was nearly melted, and tiny green shoots were beginning to appear all over the meadow. "Spring is coming!" she shouted to her friends.

Soon the days were warm and sunny again. The sparrow decided it was time to leave the burrow. "Thumbelina," he said, "you saved my life. Now I would like to help you find your mother." Thumbelina said good-bye to her field mouse friend and climbed on top of the sparrow.

Thumbelina held on tight to the sparrow's feathers as he flew high above the trees and away from the meadow.

The sparrow soared over the river where Thumbelina had traveled on her lily pad. She thought again about her home. "Do you think we will ever find my mother again?" Thumbelina asked her friend.

"Yes, but first I have something special to show you," said the sparrow. He flew deep into the forest and landed gently in a thicket. Sunlight streamed into the thicket from between the great trees above. All around them, beautiful flowers of every color blossomed.

"This must be a magical place," said Thumbelina.

And indeed it was.

No sooner had Thumbelina said this, than a beautiful lily opened before her. Out stepped a tiny boy, no bigger than a thumb. He wore a crown on his head, and he had a beautiful pair of shiny wings.

"I am the Prince of the Flowers," said the boy. "You are the kindest girl I have ever known. Come, join me, and live with us here and be the Princess of the Flowers."

With that, the meadow came alive. Tiny people stepped out of the flowers all around Thumbelina. She had never been so happy! They gave her a pair of beautiful, silvery wings, and she lived with them in the magical thicket, where it was summer all the time and never grew cold.

The Prince knew that Thumbelina missed her mother. One day he flew with Thumbelina to the cottage where her mother still lived. The woman was overjoyed to see her tiny daughter. From that day on, Thumbelina and the Prince played in the garden and told her mother stories of their magical life in the forest.

The Golden Goose

Adapted by Brian Conway
Illustrated by Karen Dugan

There once was a gentle boy called Samuel. He lived at the edge of the forest with his parents and two older brothers. His family often treated him poorly. They didn't know that he was capable of much greater things, until the day he met a strange old man in the woods near their house.

That day began as Samuel's oldest brother went to cut wood. Their mother packed a nice sweet cake and a bottle of cider for her oldest son to take into the woods. Samuel stayed home and chopped nuts.

In the woods Samuel's brother came upon a little gray man. The man kindly bid him good day and said, "Will you share your cake and cider with a tired old man? I am very hungry and thirsty."

Samuel's brother yelled at the man. "If I give you my food and drink, I won't have enough for myself," he said. "Now get out of my way!"

The brother left the man standing there and went to chop a tree. After a few strong swings, his ax slipped and hit his arm. He suffered a deep cut and could no longer continue his work. The little man saw all this happen. He smiled as Samuel's oldest brother hurried home to dress his wound.

Now the second brother was called to get the firewood. Their mother gave him sweet cake and cider, as she'd done for the oldest brother. Before long the second brother also met up with the old man in the woods. The man kindly bid him good day and said, "Would you share your cake and cider with a tired old man? I am very hungry and thirsty."

This next brother was just as selfish as the first. "If I give you my food and drink, I won't have enough for myself," he said angrily. "Now get out of my way!"

The second brother walked away and found a tree to chop. He swung so strongly with his ax, the head of the ax dropped off. It fell firmly on the brother's foot, and he, too, could no longer work. Again the little gray man smiled as he watched Samuel's second brother hobbling home.

Then young Samuel said, "Let me go cut the wood, Father."

"You know nothing about it," his father replied harshly. "But if you are so willing to get hurt, then go."

Samuel's mother handed him some cake and a jug of warm water and sent him on his way. When he reached the forest, Samuel met the little gray man as well. The man kindly bid him good day and said, "Would you kindly share some food and drink with a tired old man? I am very hungry and thirsty."

"I have only stale cake and warm water," Samuel said, "but if you don't mind that, we can eat together."

The two sat in the woods to eat. When Samuel reached for their snack, he found a magnificent slice of sweet cake and a large bottle of cider for them to share.

When they finished their tasty meal, the old man told Samuel, "You shared your goods with me, and for that I am grateful. Now you will have good luck to go with your kind heart."

The little gray man pointed at an old tree nearby. "Cut it down and you'll find something special there in its roots." Then the man walked away without another word.

Samuel swiftly cut down the old tree, and when it fell he found a goose sitting among the roots. But this was no ordinary goose. Its feathers were made of gold!

Samuel picked up the goose and hurried into town. He had to show this great goose to everyone he knew.

Samuel beamed proudly as he carried his golden goose through town. All of the townspeople gazed at the beautiful goose. He passed an inn, and the innkeeper's three curious daughters came out to see the beautiful bird. Each of the three daughters wanted one of the goose's golden feathers to keep for her own.

When Samuel stopped to show off the goose to the three sisters, the oldest sister tiptoed behind Samuel and tugged at the goose's wing. Her hand stuck there so tightly that she could not move it away. She waved to her sisters for their help.

The sisters thought that together they could surely pluck out three gold feathers. They joined hands to pull. Instead, the three sisters found they were all stuck to each other! The sisters hushed their worried squeals and scurried behind Samuel, who never noticed the girls hanging on. He marched to the next town to share his goose's beauty with anyone who wished to behold it.

Samuel hurried through a field on his way to the next town. A minister saw the procession and cried, "Have you no shame, girls? Why must you run after the boy? It's just not proper!"

The minister tried to pull the youngest girl away. All too soon he felt that he himself was stuck, and he had to run as fast as his legs could carry him to keep up with the others.

The minister's wife saw her husband running along with the three girls. She cried out in amazement, "Dear Husband, slow down! We have to be at a wedding in a few minutes!"

The minister's wife pulled on his sleeve. Then she was caught up in this silly parade, too.

They passed two farmers on a road. The minister's wife called for help, but as soon as they touched her, the farmers were pulled along, too!

Samuel hurried into the next town, with the curious party of seven behind him.

They reached a town where a king ruled with his only daughter. The young princess was so serious, so solemn, that it was believed she could not laugh. So the king sent out a proclamation. Whoever made the princess laugh would have her hand in marriage.

When Samuel heard about the princess, he took his golden goose to her, followed by the three innkeeper's daughters, the minister, the minister's wife, and the two farmers, all running in a row behind him. They quickly walked through town and made their way for the king's castle. What a sight they were!

After seeing this bumbling parade of people, the princess burst into great fits of laughter. She laughed and laughed until the king thought she might not stop.

Samuel asked the laughing princess to marry him, but before she could answer, the king stepped in. He did not want Samuel for a son-in-law, so he made up a list of conditions for Samuel.

"First," the king demanded, "you must bring me a man who can drink a whole cellarful of cider."

At once Samuel thought of the little gray man in the woods and rushed away to find him. He found the man in that same spot as before, again looking quite sad.

"What is the matter?" Samuel asked.

"It is my thirst," answered the little man. "I cannot seem to quench it. No amount of water will do, and I haven't a drop of good cider."

"Follow me," said Samuel. "You'll soon have enough to drink."

The little gray man happily drank all the cider in the king's cellar, barrel by barrel. Then Samuel approached the king and demanded his bride.

By now the king had a new condition. "Bring me a man who can eat up a mountain of bread," he demanded.

Samuel ran off to find the little gray man, who sat once again in the woods looking forlorn.

"What is the matter?" Samuel asked.

"I am so hungry," said the man. "I feel as though I could eat a mountain of bread."

Samuel smiled and answered, "I believe you shall. Follow me."

And so it was. In just one day, the little man had eaten the whole mountain of bread!

When Samuel approached the king again, the king was ready with a third demand. He thought it would be impossible for Samuel to meet this condition. "Now bring me a ship which sails on land as well as at sea," he mused. "And, as soon as I see you sail up in this vessel, you can marry my lovely daughter."

Samuel went straight for that spot in the forest. The little man was expecting him. "I have eaten a mountain of bread, and I have drunk a cellarful of cider," said the old man. "And now you shall have a special ship, too. I will share all I have with you, because you have been so kind to me."

The little man brought Samuel a ship which sailed on land as well as at sea. Samuel thanked the man, hoisted the sail, and was back at the castle in no time.

The king was astounded but now had no choice. He offered Samuel his daughter's hand.

Samuel took her hand. He asked the princess if she would marry him and share all he had to offer. She smiled so greatly that her answer was clear. They were married that day, and, throughout the kingdom, it's said, the princess has never stopped smiling since.

The Twelve Dancing Princesses

Adapted by Sarah Toast
Illustrated by Pamela R. Levy

Long ago there lived a king who had twelve beautiful and clever daughters. The princesses all slept in the same huge room, with their twelve pretty beds in a row.

The king loved his daughters dearly, but he was becoming concerned about what they did each night. Even though the king carefully locked the door of the princesses' room every night, the next morning he found the princesses tired and out of sorts. More puzzling still, their tiny silk dancing slippers were worn to shreds.

Every day, the king ordered twelve new pairs of beautiful silk shoes for his daughters. Every night he locked them in their great room, only to find a row of worn-out shoes.

The next morning, the king begged his beloved daughters to explain why they were so tired and pale, and why their dancing shoes were in shreds. But the princesses merely murmured, "Beloved Papa, we have been sleeping peacefully in our beds all night."

The king thought of a way to find out the truth. At once, he issued a proclamation declaring that the first man to solve the mystery of where the twelve princesses went to dance every night would choose a wife from among them. The king warned, however, that anyone who tried to discover the princesses' secret had only three days and three nights to succeed. After that, the suitor would be banished from the kingdom forever.

Many princes tried to solve the mystery of the king's daughters. Each prince was enchanted by the beautiful princesses. But each met the same fate: falling fast asleep after drinking a glass of wine offered by the eldest sister. Within months, all of the princes in the land had failed the test. And thus, each and every one was banished from the kingdom forever.

One day a poor soldier came limping along the road. He had been wounded and could no longer serve in battle. The soldier had no sooner sat down by the side of the road to eat some bread and cheese when an old woman appeared all dressed in rags.

"Won't you have a bite to eat with me?" said the kind soldier to the woman. He offered her half of his simple meal.

"Where are you going?" asked the woman.

"I am going to the city to find work," replied the soldier. When he saw the sad look on the old woman's face, the soldier joked, "Don't worry about me! Perhaps I can find out how the princesses wear out their shoes!"

The old woman surprised the soldier by saying, "Heed my words! Do not drink the wine that the princesses offer you. Pretend to fall asleep. And take this cloak, which will make you invisible. You can follow the princesses and discover their secret!"

The soldier didn't know what to think. He thanked the old woman politely and continued on his way. When the chill wind blew, the soldier put on the cloak and discovered that it did indeed make him invisible. He headed at once to the king's palace, where he was made welcome and introduced to the twelve sisters.

In the evening, the soldier was led to the little room next to the princesses' great room. Soon the eldest princess brought the soldier a cup of wine. He pretended to drink the sweet wine, letting it trickle down under his chin and onto his ragged scarf. Then he climbed into bed and pretended to fall asleep.

When the eldest princess heard the soldier's snores, she quietly said to her sisters, "He is as foolish as the others. Make haste. We must get ready for the ball!"

The twelve princesses chattered and laughed as they dressed in their best ball gowns and jewels and arranged each other's hair. Only the youngest princess felt uneasy. "I'm not sure what it is, but something just doesn't feel right tonight," she said.

"Don't be such a little goose," said the eldest princess fondly. "That soldier is sound asleep. He won't wake up until morning!"

When the twelve princesses were ready, they put on their new dancing shoes. Then the eldest princess tapped on her bedpost three times. The bed descended into the floor and became a long flight of stairs.

The eldest princess stepped down into the opening in the floor. One by one, her sisters followed her.

The soldier saw the princesses walk down the stairs. He sprang out of bed and threw on the cloak. Then he followed the youngest princess down the stairway.

Because his leg was lame, the soldier stumbled and stepped on the hem of the youngest princess' gown. She shrieked with alarm, "Someone has stepped on my gown!"

"Don't be so skittish," said the eldest princess. "Your dress must have caught on a nail."

The princesses and the soldier continued down many flights of stairs and along many corridors until at last they came to a passageway.

As the princesses hurried through, the soldier reached up and broke off a glittery, shiny branch of silver leaves that covered the passageway door. When the branch cracked, the youngest princess cried out again. "Did you hear that? I think someone is following us."

"Don't worry, dear," said the eldest princess. "That was just a welcoming salute from the princes who await us."

Next they came to a gleaming forest of golden trees, and then into a garden where the trees grew sparkling diamonds.

The soldier broke off a golden branch and a spray of diamonds so he would have a way to prove his story to the king. Each time he did so, the youngest princess cried out, but her sisters calmed her.

The twelve princesses hurried down a broad avenue of diamond trees to the edge of a beautiful lake. There, twelve princes awaited them in twelve little painted boats. Each princess took the hand of a handsome prince and joined him in a boat.

Unseen, the soldier just had time to sneak into the boat with the youngest princess and her companion.

On the other side of the lake stood a splendid castle. Every window was glowing with light, and fireworks lit up the sky. As the beautiful little boats approached the castle, a fanfare of trumpets announced the arrival of the twelve dancing princesses.

The princes and the princesses stepped into the castle, where beautiful music welcomed them to the ballroom. The princesses danced with their princes for half the night.

The soldier joined the dancing unseen and unnoticed. The youngest princess did notice, however, when the soldier took a small sip from her cup of wine.

"Someone has tasted my drink!" she exclaimed.

"Nonsense, little sister. Come back and enjoy the dancing!" said her older sisters in reply. "The night is almost over!"

Soon, the night ended and the princes rowed the twelve princesses back across the lake. This time the soldier rode with the eldest sister. The princesses said good-bye and promised to return the next night.

Then the princesses hurried back the way they had come, through the garden of diamonds and the forests of gold and of silver. They retraced their steps through the corridors and up the staircases.

The princesses were so tired that they slowed down at the top of the last set of stairs. The soldier was able to dash ahead of them, throw off his cloak, and jump into his bed.

The tired princesses dragged themselves into their room while the eldest princess checked on the soldier to be sure he was asleep. "We are safe!" she said. With that, all twelve sisters fell fast asleep.

The next morning the soldier visited the king in his chambers.

"Good soldier," said the king, "many good men have come before me and have failed to solve this mystery. Have you discovered where my lovely daughters dance their shoes to shreds every night?"

"Your Highness, I have," said the soldier. "They go down a hidden staircase. Then they walk through three enchanted forests to a beautiful lake. Twelve princes take them across the lake to a castle where they dance the night away."

The king couldn't believe the soldier's story until the soldier showed him the golden cup and the branches of silver, gold, and diamonds. Then the king summoned his daughters, who at last admitted the truth. The eldest princess laughed and said, "I didn't think it could be done, but the soldier certainly has outwitted us!"

The king told the soldier that he could choose one of the princesses to be his wife. It didn't take the soldier very long to make his decision. He had already decided that he liked the eldest princess best. She was clever and spirited as well as beautiful. For her part, the princess thought the soldier was clever and kind.

The soldier was given royal chambers and royal garments to wear. He and the eldest princess were married, and the wedding guests happily danced the night away.

George and the Dragon

Adapted by Brian Conway
Illustrated by Tammie Speer Lyon

Before St. George became the patron saint of England, he was just George, a boy who liked to pretend he was a great and brave knight. George lived among the fairies for much of his youth. The queen of the fairies had taken him in as a baby, and the fairies raised him as their own. As he grew up, they taught him to be brave and strong, calm and courteous, quick and clever. They taught him to be a noble knight and prepared him for all the adventures he would soon have.

"Your journey starts today," the queen of the fairies told him one day. "You have many adventures before you now. The world is filled with monsters to be slain and battles to be fought. You'll meet kings and paupers, wizards and witches, evil princes and kind princesses."

"Yes, Your Majesty," George bowed before the queen. He was very fond of her. He was sad to leave the Land of the Fairies, but he was not afraid. He knew he had to go.

"Always remember one thing," the queen added, tapping George's silver battle helmet. "Your greatest weapon, George, is your mind."

George traveled many weeks, through many wonderful kingdoms.

"I am a brave and noble knight," he told anyone who asked.

They all said they'd like to hear about his adventures. Sadly, he had none to tell as yet, so he asked them to show him the way of greatest peril. Everyone without hesitation pointed toward the kingdom of Silene. They uttered not a single word more.

As George approached Silene, he noticed the land changed from lush and green to desolate and dark. It seemed the ground had been crossed by fire. There was no grass, only the darkest mud. The trees were bare and black, and a foul stench filled the air.

George walked through this stark land for most of a full day. He did not see a soul—not a bird, not a squirrel, and certainly not a single person.

George finally saw a castle in the distance. A high, solid wall enclosed the castle and the small city around it. The gate was closed up tight. Again, George saw no one around. He got closer and saw a young lady. She crept quietly through the gate.

"Excuse me, my dear lady," he called after her.

"Quiet!" she hushed him. "Have you no sense? You would do well to leave here now and never return."

"But I am a brave knight here to help you," George whispered.

"Alas, sir," the woman replied, "you are but one man. You cannot help."

George looked her in the eyes. "It is my destiny," he told the woman. "I will not go until I have done all I can, even if it costs me my life."

"I am Princess Sabra," she said. "Come with me."

They tiptoed through what was once a deep, green forest. Sabra explained why the kingdom lived in such fear.

A fearful dragon had lived in the kingdom for many years, she told him. The horrible beast had ravaged the land. Many men had tried to slay the dragon, but his sharp claws, his vast flapping wings, and his hot breath of fire made the dragon impossible to reach, let alone kill.

The people had moved within the castle walls for protection. But soon the dragon had run out of animals to eat.

"If you do not give me two of your sheep each day," the dragon roared, "I will come through those walls for my breakfast!" So each morning, as the sun rose, so rose the dragon, looking for its breakfast.

"We gave up our last two sheep this very morning," said the princess. "Tomorrow we shall have nothing to give the dragon, and we will perish."

"Then I have arrived at the right time," said George bravely.

Sabra led him to a cave in the dark forest. "To slay the dragon," Sabra told George, "we need help. That is why we are here."

In the cave there lived a wise old hermit. Some said he was a sorcerer more than 900 years old, but no one knew for sure. Sabra and George crept up to the hermit, who stared into his fire. He did not turn to look at them, but he spoke as if he knew they were coming.

> Long ago, it was told,
> Two brave knights would come to know,
> The only way to save the rest:
> The Serpent's weakness in his breath.

With those words, an ancient hourglass appeared at their feet.

George did not understand. He asked the strange little man, but the hermit would speak no more.

When George and Sabra left the cave, it was already dark. They knew they must hurry to find the dragon while the beast was still sleeping.

"What do we do with this ancient timepiece?" Sabra sighed.

George remembered what the queen of fairies had told him. His best weapon, she had said, was his mind. He studied the hourglass closely. The tiny blue grains of sand fell through to the bottom of the glass one by one. Each bit of sand looked like a magic crystal frozen in time.

They arrived at the lake. George and Sabra walked softly through the fog so they would not be heard. The sands in the hourglass dropped with every careful step.

George thought he might like to have his sword at this moment, but he felt he must have faith in what the Queen had said. He truly did not know what would happen at the dragon's lair.

"The time left in the hourglass will lead us," George whispered. "We must wait until all the sand has dropped through, then we should know what to do."

The smell as they approached the lair was horrible. No one had ever been so close to the dragon before, and not a soul had ever been brave enough, or perhaps foolish enough, to dare enter the dragon's lair. George was afraid but knew he must be brave for Sabra. He was a brave knight, he told himself.

George set his shield near the sleeping dragon's head. There they were protected from the dragon's snores, when hot blasts of fire poured from his scaly nose. They watched the icy blue sands tick away, and they waited quietly as to not wake the sleeping beast.

Suddenly the dragon stirred. Surely the dragon would find them before they could escape.

George stood his ground and closely watched the mighty dragon.

The dragon raised himself up and rubbed his slimy eyes. As George watched the dragon rise, the very last grain of sand was dropping through. At that very moment, the huge dragon stretched and yawned a terrible, fiery yawn.

George knew what must be done. He threw the hourglass up, up, up to the dragon's yawning mouth. It shattered on the dragon's slithering tongue in a cloud of icy mist.

Now our two heroes had sorely angered the dragon. He looked down to see them. Both George and Sabra ducked behind the shield. The dragon reared back to hurl a fiery blast at them. But only cool ice and soft snow came from the dragon's mouth. The dragon took a deep breath, certain the furnace inside of him would melt the ice.

But, the hermit's magic had changed the dragon. His mouth shut tight with frozen ice, the once-fearsome dragon jumped into the deep, warm lake. Only there could he keep from freezing from the inside out.

George and Sabra had saved the kingdom. They arrived at the castle to hear great cries of joy and triumph.

The king offered George all he had in thanks, but George wanted no payment for his deeds.

"I have many more adventures left to face," George told the people. "They are my greatest reward."

THE
END